MR ARCHIMEDES' BATH

To Pirée Hartley with thanks

Copyright © PAMELA ALLEN 1980
ISBN 0 370 30258 3
Printed and bound in Singapore for
The Bodley Head Ltd, 9 Bow Street,
London WC2E 7AL
by Kyodo-Shing Loong Printing Industries (Pte) Ltd
First published in Sydney by William Collins Publishers Pty Ltd 1980
First published in Great Britain 1980

MR ARCHIMEDES' BATH

PAMELA ALLEN

THE BODLEY HEAD

LONDON SYDNEY TORONTO

Mr Archimedes' bath always overflowed.

And Mr Archimedes always had to clean up the mess.

"Can anyone tell me where all this water came from?"

Mr Archimedes decided to find out.
He put just a little water in the bath,
as he always did, and this time
he measured the depth.

But the water rose.

"Where did all this water come from?"
bellowed Mr Archimedes.

"I don't know," said Kangaroo.

"It's not my fault," said Goat.

"I didn't do it," said Wombat.

But when Mr Archimedes measured it again, he found the water had gone down. Mr Archimedes was puzzled.

"Somebody must be doing this," he shouted. "Where's it gone?"

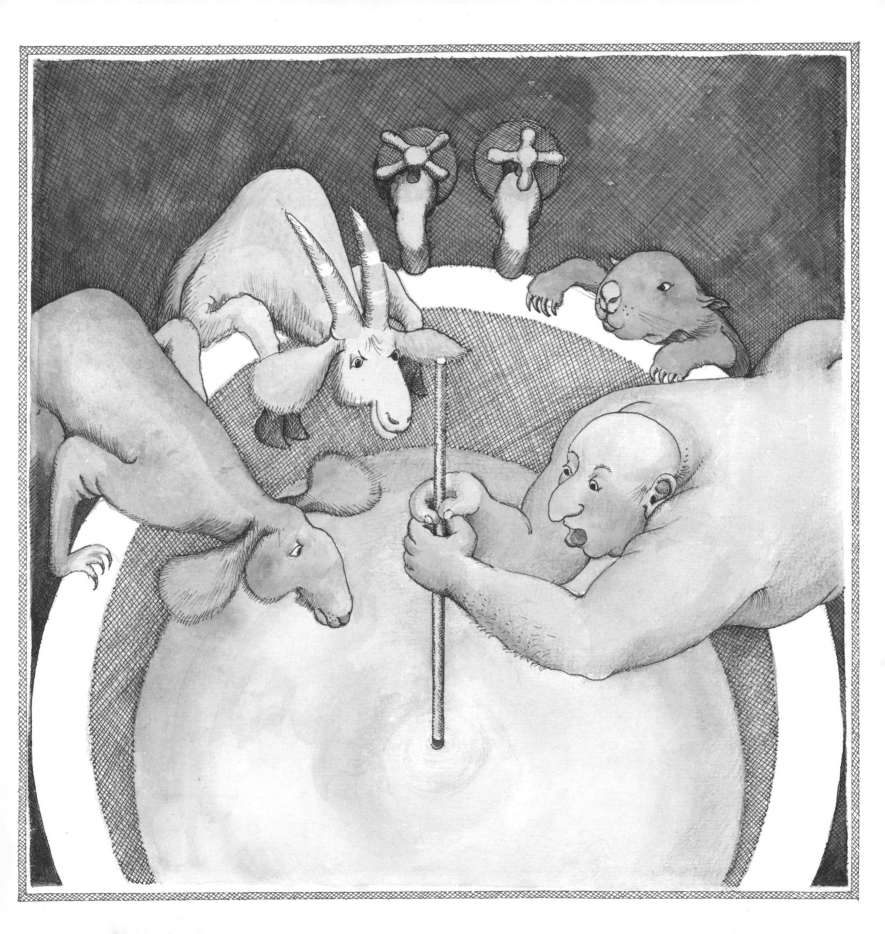

"Maybe it is you, Kangaroo.
You stay out and we shall see
if it happens again."

The water rose.

When Mr Archimedes measured it,
he found it had gone down again.
"Now let's see what happens when
you are left out, Goat."

Again the water rose.
That left only Wombat to blame.
Mr Archimedes was angry.
"Get out and stay out," he shouted.

But the same thing happened.
Who could be responsible if it
wasn't Kangaroo and it wasn't Goat
and it wasn't Wombat?

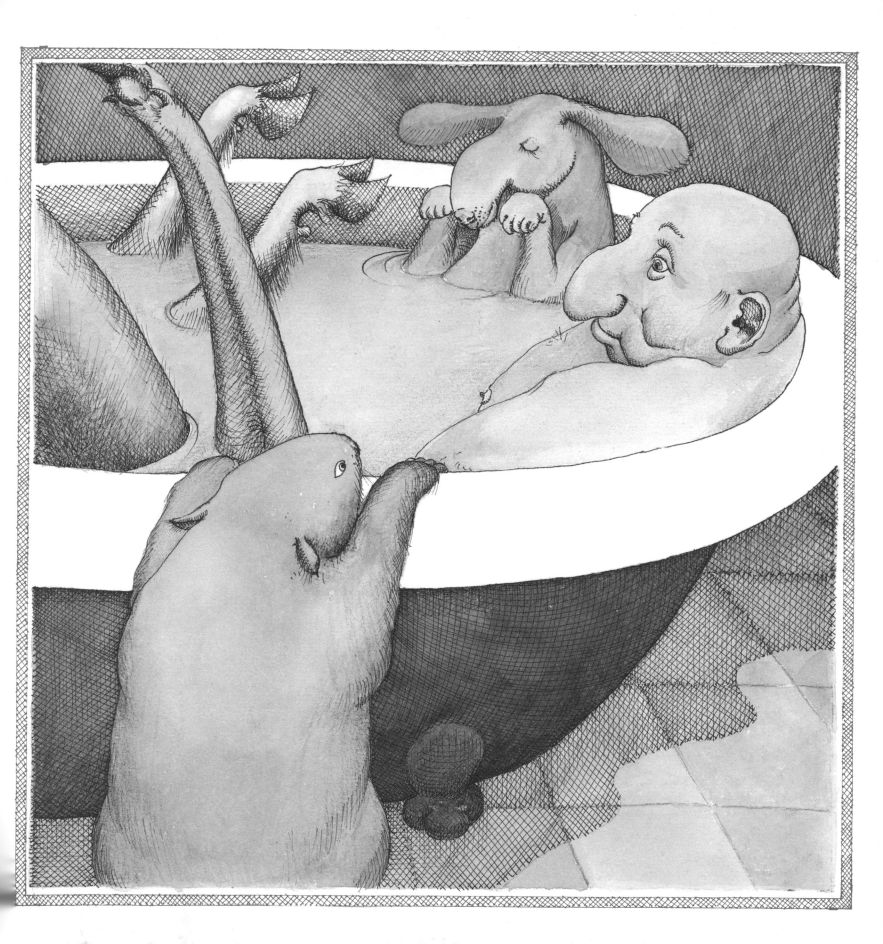

Could it be Mr Archimedes?
The friends decided he should have
his bath all to himself.
He climbed in,

and the water rose.

He climbed out, and the water fell
until there was just the same amount
Mr Archimedes had put in.

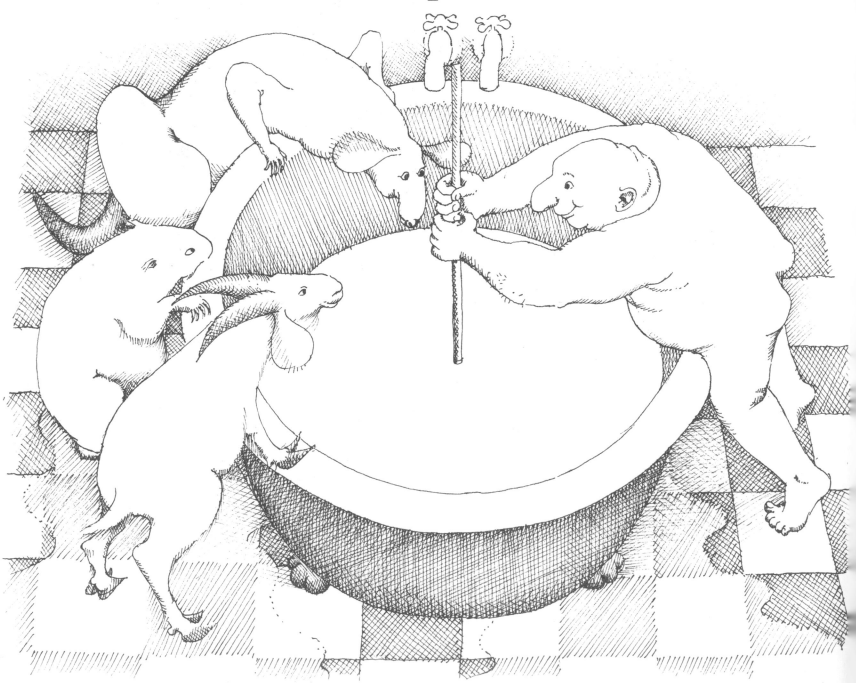

Mr Archimedes got so excited that
he jumped in and out, in and out,
to make the water go up and down.

"EUREKA!

I've found it, I've found it!" he shouted.
"Jump in everyone!"

And the bath overflowed.

"See," said Mr Archimedes.
"*We* make the water go up.
There are just too many of us
in the bath, that's all!"

The friends had so much fun that night, jumping in and out, making the water go up and down, that they made more mess than ever before.